HANNAH MAE
THE LITTLE
PELICAN
OF
SARASOTA BAY

by Gladys Dorfman

Published in the United States by
Hannah Mae Enterprises, Inc.
P.O. Box 81143
Springfield, MA 01138-1143
Text copyright ©1998 by Gladys Dorfman
Illustrations copyright ©1999 by Gladys Dorfman
Third Printing 2004

Printed in the United States by Arrow Printing. Bemidji, Minnesota.

Publisher's Cataloging-in-Publication
(Provided by Quality Books, Inc.)
Dorfman, Gladys.
    Hannah Mae the little pelican of Sarasota Bay/
    by Gladys Dorfman. -- 1st ed.
    p. cm.
    LCCN: 99-71679
    ISBN: 0-9671111-0-2
    Summary: A young pelican named Hannah Mae injures her wing,
    so her pelican friend Cappie finds a way to alert the Pelican Man,
    who treats her at his bird sanctuary.

    1. Pelicans--Juvenile fiction. 2. Sarasota Bay (Fla.)--Juvenile fiction.
    3. Wildlife rescue--Florida--Juvenile fiction. I. Title.

    PZ7.D727478Han 1999   [E]
                    QBI99-494

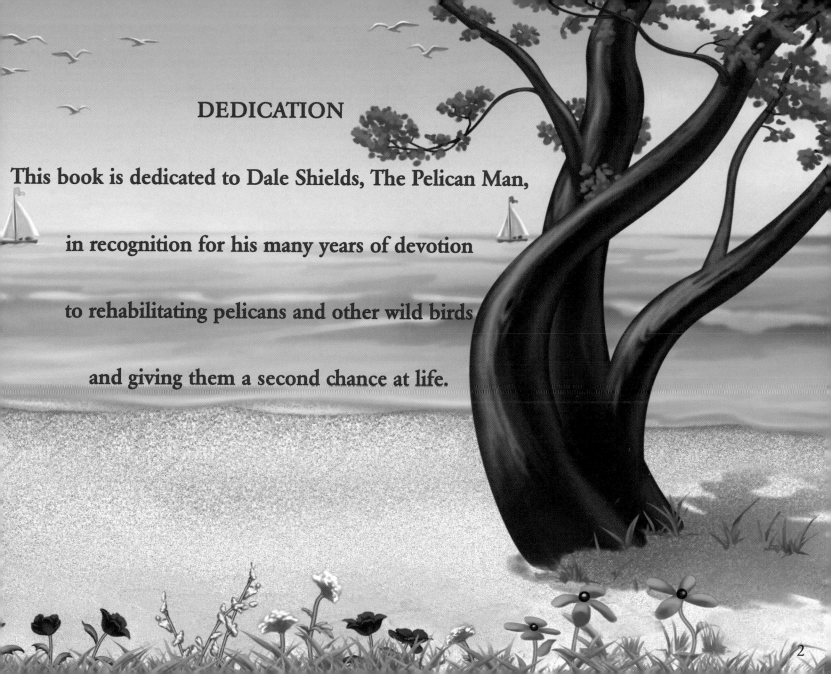

DEDICATION

This book is dedicated to Dale Shields, The Pelican Man,

in recognition for his many years of devotion

to rehabilitating pelicans and other wild birds

and giving them a second chance at life.

PECK! PECK! PECK! Hannah Mae, the little pelican of Sarasota Bay, was pecking her way out of her shell.

She pecked and pecked
until she made a hole
large enough to
crawl out.

4

Hannah Mae grew fast. Soon she was covered with white downy feathers. When she was five weeks old, she was old enough to be left alone. Her parents would fly off and return only to feed her.

Hannah Mae had a friend named Cappie. He was an older pelican. Hannah Mae liked to waddle down to the edge of the water and watch Cappie dive for fish. One day, as Hannah Mae was watching Cappie, she stepped out onto a log. Suddenly, the log began to move faster and faster out into the bay.

When the log reached the middle of the bay there
was a loud SPLASH! SPLASH! SPLASH!

Up popped three playful dolphins. One
big manatee and two baby manatees swam by.
Hannah Mae was having fun watching the dolphins and
manatees. By the end of the day, the log had floated to
the opposite shore. Suddenly, there was a
loud BANG!

8

The log had hit
against a large rock.
Hannah Mae was thrown into
the air and landed on her wing,
and it began to hurt.
She picked herself up and
waddled onto the shore.

Cappie was flying overhead and saw
what had happened. He flew down and
built Hannah Mae a nice warm nest. He
stayed with her through the night. When
the sun began to rise, he flew away.

Cappie saw a man with a blue cap on his head. He had just finished putting a bandage on an injured pelican's foot and was putting the bird into his truck.

Cappie flew down, took the man's cap and flew away with it.

The man chased after Cappie
until he saw Hannah Mae.

11

He picked her up
and bandaged
her wing.

He put Hannah Mae into his truck, and Cappie sat down beside her. As they were driving along, Hannah Mae's mother and father were flying overhead and saw Hannah Mae. They flew down and sat near her in the truck. The man was taking Hannah Mae to his bird sanctuary. The man was called the Pelican Man because he took care of injured pelicans and other birds.

The doctor at the bird sanctuary repaired
Hannah Mae's wing. Cappie and Hannah Mae's parents
stayed with her until she was better. Then they flew away,
but came to visit her each day.

When Hannah Mae's wing had almost healed, the Pelican Man took her around the sanctuary and showed her all the other injured birds. 18

Hannah Mae's injured wing never grew as large as her other wing. She was unable to fly, so she stayed at the sanctuary with the Pelican Man. She had a nice nest to sleep on, a swimming pool to swim in, and she was well fed. She also made lots of new friends.

One of her new friends was Squirrel. Hannah Mae and Squirrel liked to follow the Pelican Man around the sanctuary. Sometimes Blue the blue jay or Woody the woodpecker would fly down and sit on the Pelican Man's cap.

One day, Hannah Mae and Squirrel watched the Pelican Man take Gussie the goose and some other geese for a walk. After their walk, the Pelican Man returned them to their fenced-in area. As he called their names, they entered the area one by one. All of a sudden, Gussie ran to the front of the line. The Pelican Man told her to go back and wait until her name was called. Gussie obeyed.

When they were all inside their fenced-in area, the Pelican Man bent over and Gussie gave him a kiss good night.

Hannah Mae and Squirrel followed the Pelican Man as he said good night to all the other birds. When he got to Angie, the talking crow, Angie looked sad. She said to the Pelican Man, "No Fair." "I know," said the Pelican Man. "It's not fair that you're injured and have to live in a cage." He visited with Angie for a while and then said good night to her.

22

If you ever visit the bird sanctuary at Sarasota Bay, you
might see Squirrel, or Blue the blue jay, or Woody the woodpecker. You
might hear Angie the talking crow say, "No Fair." You might even see Hannah Mae.
She has a bench named after her that you can sit on. It reads:

Hannah Mae The Little Pelican of Sarasota Bay

HANNAH MAE
THE LITTLE PELICAN
OF SARASOTA BAY

THE BROWN PELICAN

Colonies of brown pelicans make their nests in mangrove trees on islands off Sarasota Bay. Where there are no mangrove trees, pelicans sometimes nest on the ground. Adult pelicans normally lay two or three eggs in late winter or early spring. For about thirty days, the parents take turns incubating the eggs under their warm feet. Pelican chicks at birth are featherless and grey-skinned. They grow very rapidly. Within ten days, they are covered with white downy feathers and resemble little snowballs. Baby pelicans rely on their parents both for food and for protection from predators and the environment.

Pelicans change colors constantly. Colors vary according to breeding cycle, season and age. At five weeks old, baby pelicans shed their fluffy white down and begin to grow small brownish feathers on their wings. Now the pelican parents leave their grown chicks and return to the nest only to feed them. By ten weeks, young pelicans have white bellies and brown feathers on their heads, necks and wings. Pelicans between ten and twelve weeks old, now almost as large as their parents, learn to fly.

When the young pelican is two years old, its head, neck and wings are brown. Gradually, its white belly turns brown. By the time the pelican is three, its head, neck and belly have turned a brownish-grey. By the fourth year, the pelican's belly is grey and neck is brown. Its head now begins to turn white.

At four or five years of age, the adult pelican begins to mate. The pelican's head feathers turn yellow during courtship. Its neck is white and a diamond-shaped area of the upper chest turns yellow. Eventually, its head and the diamond-shaped feathers on the chest turn white, and the back of its neck turns brown. These colors remain essentially the same throughout the thirty year life span of the pelican.

The author thanks Roc Goudreau and Gary LaCoste for their collaboration in perfecting the drawings used in this book.

Special thanks to Dale Shields, "The Pelican Man," for graciously providing information about the brown pelican.